FEROCIOUS FLUFFITY

words by
ERICA S. PERL

pictures by
HENRY COLE

A Mighty Bite-y Class Pet

Abrams Books for Young Readers
New York

The illustrations in this book were made with watercolor.

Cataloging-in-Publication Data has been applied for and may be obtained from the Library of Congress

ISBN 978-1-4197-2182-3

Printed and bound in China
10 9 8 7 6 5 4 3 2 1

Abrams Books for Young Readers are available at special discounts when purchased in quantity for premiums and promotions as well as fundraising or educational use. Special editions can also be created to specification. For details, contact specialsales@abramsbooks.com or the address below.

ABRAMS
THE ART OF BOOKS SINCE 1949
115 West 18th Street
New York, NY 10011
www.abramsbooks.com

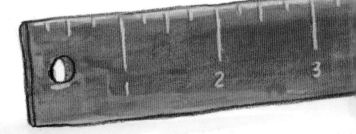

To Fran McCrackin, Tawana Franklin, Jason Jones, and the
ferociously fabulous Janney community. Go, Jaguars!
—E.S.P.

For Joanie, with smooches.
—H.C.

The box was big and tall and wide.
Could there be a pet inside?
Children pushed and shoved to see.
"Awwwwwww!!!" they cried out happily.

"She's so tiny!" "She's so sweet!"
"Such cute whiskers!" "Such cute feet!"
Mr. Drake said, "Look—don't touch.
She's too little. It's too much."

Though the children nodded yes,
Did they mean it? Take a guess.
Everyone in Room 2-D
Dreamed of holding Fluffity.

So one day when Mr. Drake
Overslept (quite by mistake),
All his students yelled, "Hooray!
We can take her out today!"

No one's sure who held her first.
Things got bad. Then things got worse.
She was tiny. She was cute.
She was also quite a brute.

She bit Eddie.

She bit Bert.

She bit Whitby.
"Yee-ouch!" It hurt!

She bit Julia

and Jamal.

Bit them.
Bit them.
Bit them all.

Children screamed, and children ran:
Zander, Zara, Sydney, Stan,
Kevin K., and Kevin B.
At their heels was Fluffity.

First she chased them down the hall,
Through the gym, and up a wall.

Where to run to? Where to hide?
Library! They dashed inside.

Meanwhile, back in Room 2-D,
Mr. Drake said, "Woe is me!
Where can all my students be?
Hey—and where is Fluffity?!"

She bit Ruthie.

She bit Rose.

She bit "Dathan" on the "dose."

She bit Perrin,

Pam,

and Paul.

Bit them.
Bit them.
Bit them all.

As she bit and bit some more,
Mr. Drake burst through the door.
"Children! Are you all okay?"

But their warning came too late.
Mr. Drake now met his fate.
Quick as lightning, Fluffity
Opened wide . . .

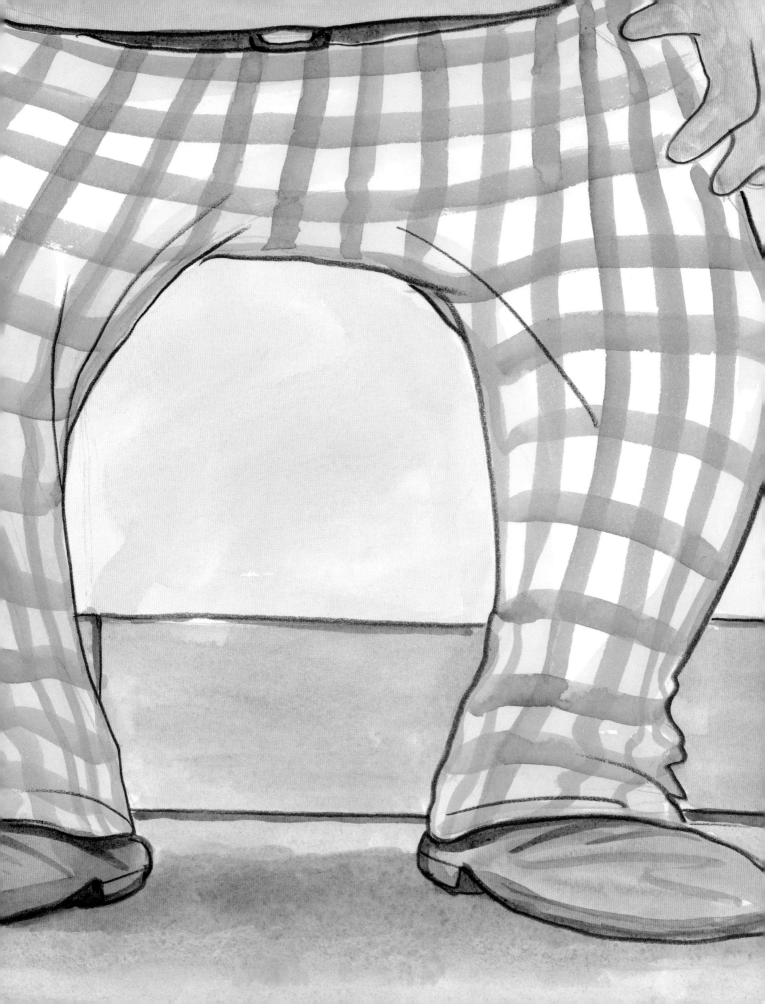

. . . and bit his knee
(Hanging on tenaciously).

Kids tried tickling.

Kids tried toys.

Kids tried making
LOTS OF NOISE!

All the kids agreed that they
Learned a thing or two that day:
Get to know your pet *before*
Opening her cage's door.

Fluffity, they came to learn,
Had lots of energy to burn.
Exercise helped her to be
MUCH less prone to injury!

Now the kids in Room 2-D
Take good care of Fluffity.
So much so that Mr. Drake
Forgave them for their big mistake.

In fact, he just agreed to let
His students get one more class pet.
Come by at two. They're having cake
And welcoming their new pet,

Jake.